To Ella & Fialena—Always Growing
Love, Maryann

STERLING CHILDREN'S BOOKS
New York

An Imprint of Sterling Publishing Co., Inc.
1166 Avenue of the Americas
New York, NY 10036

ISBN 978-1-4549-2704-4

Distributed in Canada by Sterling Publishing Co., Inc.
c/o Canadian Manda Group, 664 Annette Street
Toronto, Ontario M6S 2C8, Canada
Distributed in the United Kingdom by GMC Distribution Services
Castle Place, 166 High Street, Lewes, East Sussex BN7 1XU, England
Distributed in Australia by NewSouth Books,
University of New South Wales, Sydney, NSW 2052, Australia

For information about custom editions, special sales, and premium and corporate purchases,
please contact Sterling Special Sales at 800-805-5489 or specialsales@sterlingpublishing.com.

Manufactured in China

Lot #:
2 4 6 8 10 9 7 5 3 1
01/19

sterlingpublishing.com

Cover and interior design by Irene Vandervoort
Title lettering by Maryann Cocca-Leffler

The artwork for this book was created using gouache, colored pencil, and collage elements.

GROWING Season

Maryann Cocca-Leffler

STERLING CHILDREN'S BOOKS

New York

Best friends El and Jo were the smallest students in the class.

Even their names were short.

El and Jo were always together.

They sat next to each other in their "just the
right size" desks . . .

and helped each other reach the unreachable.

You're like
two peas
in a pod.

Gardening
Center

On picture day, El and Jo were front and center.

They played perfect twin elves in the
Holiday Show . . .

and were small enough to share the special
reading chair.

But in springtime,
something BIG happened.

When it was Jo's turn to water the plants,
she didn't need El's help.

And Jo's "just the right size" desk was not the right size anymore.

El felt smaller every day.

On the last day of school, Mr. Diaz told everyone to take a flower home and care for it over the summer.

All the kids rushed to the windowsill.

They reached over tiny El, grabbing all the flower pots with colorful blooms.

There was only one pot left for El.
It was small with no flowers at all.
"I know just how you feel, little plant." said El.

Mr. Diaz leaned in. "El, that's an aster plant. Aster means 'star.'"

"It's no star. It's just a little, plain green plant," said El.

"Just you wait! In time, it will grow and have beautiful purple blooms," said Mr. Diaz.

El was not so sure.

Jo looked over at El's sad plant, and then at her own.

"You can have my zinnia plant," said Jo. "I'll be at my grandma's all summer anyway."

"I'll plant Aster and Zinnia side by side," said El.
"They will be best friends—just like us!" said Jo.
El smiled.

When El got home, she carefully planted the flowers in the garden.

It was growing season—all summer long, she watered them . . .

and talked to them.

Summer became the waiting season.
El waited for Aster to bloom.

And she waited for Jo to return.

On the last day of summer, Jo came home!

El and Jo ran straight to the garden . . . and suddenly stopped.

Something BIG had happened.

Aster had finally bloomed . . .

aster

zinnia

and so had EL!

PLANT LIFE CYCLES

ANNUAL FLOWERS are plants that have a life cycle that lasts only one year. They grow from seeds, bloom, and produce seeds, but then the roots, stems, and leaves die. Many annuals give your garden colorful blooms all summer long, but they must be replanted each spring. Zinnia, marigolds, and petunias are annuals.

MR. D FUN FACT:
Marigolds have a distinctive smell. Plant them in a vegetable garden to keep the bugs away!

PERENNIAL FLOWERS are plants that will bloom for many seasons. They usually spread and multiply on their own. The good news is you don't have to replant them in the spring, but, when they bloom, the flowers don't last long. Different perennials bloom at different times during the season. Columbine flowers bloom in the spring. Asters are late bloomers and don't bloom until late summer or fall.

MR. D FUN FACT:
Did you know that peonies can live for over 100 years?

BIENNIAL FLOWERS are plants that require two years to complete their life cycle. The first year the plant just grows some leaves. In the second year, the flowers bloom, form seeds, and then the entire plant dies. Foxgloves and hollyhocks are good examples of biennials.

MR. D FUN FACT:
When you plant foxgloves indoors (like we did) they will bloom the first year!

MR. D FUN FACT:
Dahlias are tender perennials from Mexico and South America. Their flowers can grow as big as a dinner plate.

TENDER PERENNIAL FLOWERS are plants that can be either an annual or a perennial depending on the local climate. Sometimes plants in warmer climates are perennials, but the same plant will be an annual in a colder climate. Impatiens and some geraniums are examples of tender perennials.